PUFFIN 🐧 Presents

Stegosaurus as Himself

MUNGO as the Hero

SAM as the Villain

MUNGO AND THE DINOSAUR ISLAND!

In glorious TECHNICOLOUR!

TIMOTHY **KNAPMAN**
as the writer

ADAM **STOWER**
as the illustrator

• FILMED IN SUPER-STOMP-AROUND-SURROUND-SOUND • WARNING – CERTAIN SEQUENCES ONLY SUITABLE FOR CHILDREN • NO DINOSAURS WERE HARMED DURING THE MAKING OF THIS BOOK •

PUFFIN BOOKS

Published by the Penguin Group:

London, New York, Australia, Canada, India,
Ireland, New Zealand and South Africa

Penguin Books Ltd, Registered Offices:
80 Strand, London WC2R 0RL, England

puffinbooks.com

First published 2008

1 3 5 7 9 10 8 6 4 2

Text copyright © Timothy Knapman, 2008
Illustrations copyright © Adam Stower, 2008
All rights reserved

The moral right of the author and illustrator
has been asserted

Made and printed in China

ISBN: 978-0-141-50110-9

This is Mungo.
Dinosaurs are his favourite
thing in the whole
wide world.

He's chosen a book from the library called

**THE AMAZING SECRET
OF THE LOST ISLAND.**

It's all about an old film.
And this is the story it tells . . .

WANTED

SCARFACE SAM SNAFFLER
WICKED WILD-ANIMAL HUNTER
IF YOU SEE THIS MAN,
DO NOT APPROACH HIM!
(HE SMELLS REVOLTING!)

THE LEAKY TUB

RAPSCALLION GA...

Scarface Sam Snaffler and his rascally rapscallion crew were all at sea in uncharted waters looking for the **LOST ISLAND**.

THA-DUNK!

"Hooray!" cried the crew.
"We've found it."

Welcome to the LOST ISLAND

"Righto, you rascally rapscallions!" said Scarface Sam. "We're here to steal the rarest creature in the whole wide world:

the Utterly Fluttery Butterfly."

"What?" said the crew.
"We've come ALL this way to catch a BUTTERFLY?"

"There it is," said Scarface Sam.
"AFTER IT!"

The hunters chased *the Utterly Fluttery Butterfly* across clacking crabs,

OUCH!

through slip-slidey swamps,

YEESSH!

and into prickly-tickly jungle.

OO-AH-OO!

Until, at last, *the Utterly Fluttery Butterfly*

settled on a great grey rock . . .

"*FLAMING FOSSILS!*" cried Scarface Sam. "*DINOSAURS!*"

Scarface Sam was right, there were dinosaurs EVERYWHERE.

"Quick, lads, catch them," he cried. "Cram them into those cages.

Who needs an *Utterly Fluttery Butterfly*

when there are DINOSAURS about?"

But little did the hunters
know that SOMEONE had been
watching them ever since they'd
arrived on the island.

Someone called
STEGOSAURUS,
the bravest dinosaur
who ever lived!

"Those rascally rapscallions
won't get away with this!"
he cried, grabbing a vine
and swinging over
to his friend, Brachiosaurus.

"Sorry about this," he said,
and he bit Brachiosaurus
on his big dinosaur bottom.

"YEEEE-OOOUCHH!"

bellowed Brachiosaurus. And he started
a deafening dinosaur stampede.

"Come on, everyone,"
said Stegosaurus.
"Let's drive these rascally
rapscallions into the sea!"

Looking at the picture in the book, Mungo could
almost see the dinosaurs moving and hear the
rumbling thunder of their charging feet.

"Oh, how I wish," he thought, "how I wish
that the dinosaurs were alive and real and here with me now."

He wished SO hard that he didn't notice the jungly vines creeping and curling out of the book and tangling and twisting round his bed.

And the harder Mungo wished, the louder
the rumbling thunder seemed to grow,
as if the dinosaurs were getting closer,

and closer,

and closer until . . .

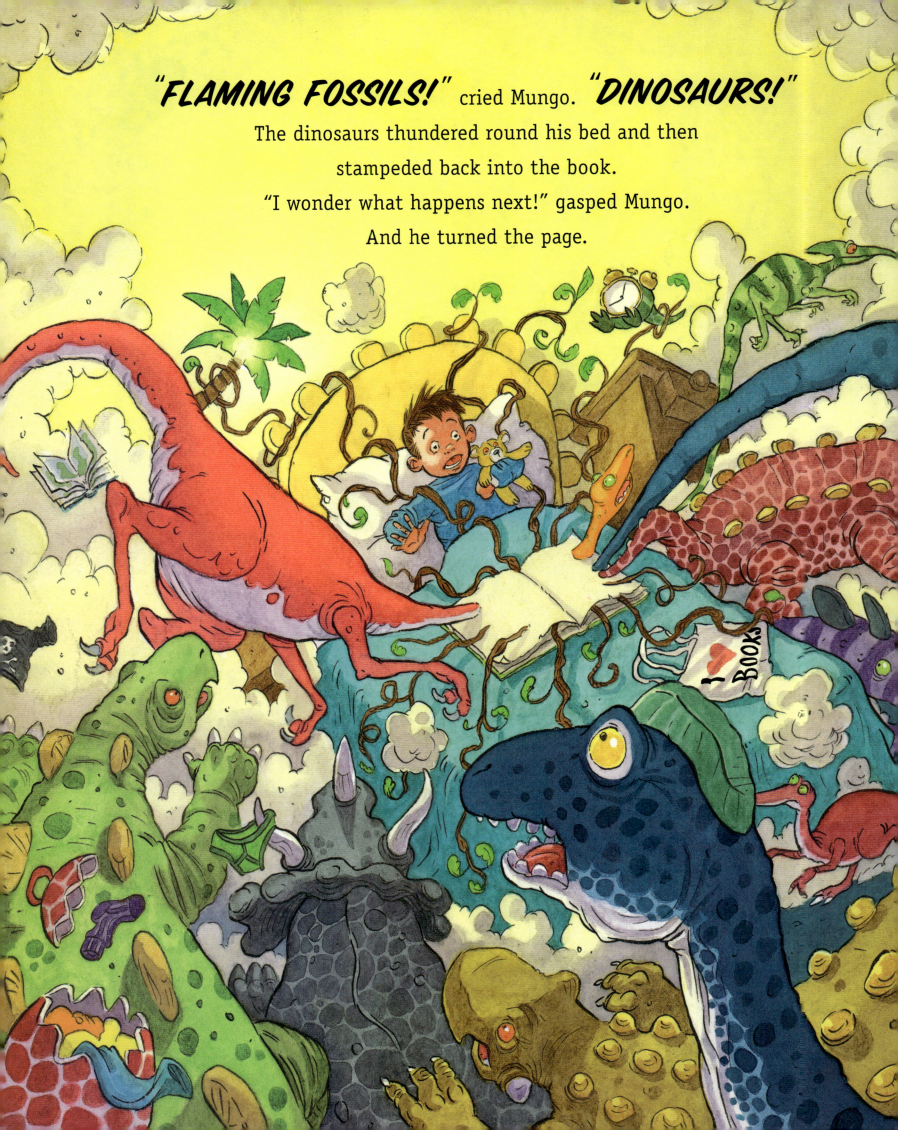

"FLAMING FOSSILS!" cried Mungo. "DINOSAURS!"
The dinosaurs thundered round his bed and then
stampeded back into the book.
"I wonder what happens next!" gasped Mungo.
And he turned the page.

"**NOOOOOOO!**" cried Stegosaurus.

"Now look what you've done! We're supposed to chase the hunters away but you turned the page too soon!

Now I'm left behind and the hunters are squashing and squishing my friends into tiny cages.

THE WHOLE STORY'S GOING WRONG!"

"Oh, crumbs," said Mungo.

There was nothing for it.

Mungo grabbed hold of Stegosaurus

and the last of the jungly vines

and together they swung out of the room . . .

. . . and into the book!

They dangled from a pterodactyl –

Slid down one diplodocus

and up another –

BOUNCED

on a triceratops –

And landed on the beach.

"WE'RE SAVED!"

cried the dinosaurs.

But before Mungo
could set them free, a huge
shadow loomed over him . . .

"YEE-OUCH!" cried Scarface Sam.

"There's something in my underpants!"

"STEGOSAURUS!" cried Mungo.

"Don't mind me," said Stegosaurus.

"I'm just a nipper!"

"AFTER THEM!" bellowed Scarface Sam.

But their path was blocked by a great grey rock.
"There's no escape this time," said Scarface Sam.
"That'll teach little boys to go meddling in story books."
And he smiled wickedly.

But not for long.

"*TYRANNOSAURUS REX!*"

shrieked the hunters.

And they were in their boat and rowing away from the
LOST ISLAND so fast they were just a blur.

"I don't think we'll be hearing from them in a hurry," said Stegosaurus. "Not unless they want to be tea for a T-Rex!" said Mungo.

"Thank you, Mungo, you daring **DINOSAUR DEFENDER,"** said Stegosaurus. "You saved my friends AND made sure our book ends properly!"

When Mungo's mum came in to turn off the light, Mungo was fast asleep and dreaming of rascally rapscallions, **LOST ISLANDS**...

...and the night the **DINOSAURS** went thundering around his bedroom!

THE END

To Zachary and Joshua, with love – T.K.

For Mary-saurus Rex, with love from Dad-plodocus x – A.S.